RUBÁIYÁT
of
OMAR KHAYYAM

A
PERSONAL SELECTION
FROM THE FIVE EDITIONS
of

EDWARD FITZGERALD

ILLUSTRATIONS
EDMUND DULAC and WILLY POGÁNY

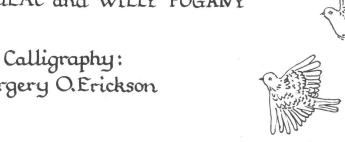

Calligraphy:
Margery O. Erickson

ISBN 0-9699121-1-0

'These pearls of thought in Persian Gulfs were bred,
Each softly lucent as a rounded moon;
The diver Omar plucked them from their bed,
FitzGerald strung them on an English thread...'

James Russell Lowell, in a copy of *The Rubáiyát*

OMAR KHAYYÁM

THE ASTRONOMER-POET OF PERSIA

Omar Khayyám was born at Naishápúr in Khorassán in the latter half of our Eleventh, and died within the First Quarter of our Twelfth, Century. The slender Story of his Life is curiously twined about that of two other very considerable Figures in their Time and Country: one of them, Hasan al Sabbáh, whose very Name has lengthen'd down to us as a terrible Synonym for Murder: and the other (who tells the Story of all Three) Nizám ul Mulk, Vizyr to Alp the Lion and Malik Shah, Son and Grandson of

Toghrul Beg the Tartar, who had wrested Persia from the feeble Successor of Mahmúd the Great, and founded that Seljukian Dynasty which finally roused Europe into the Crusades. This Nizám ul Mulk, in his *Wasyat* ~ or *Testament* ~ which he wrote and left as a Memorial for future Statesmen ~ relates the following, as quoted in the *Calcutta Review*, No. LIX, from Mirkhond's *History of the Assassins*.

"One of the greatest of the wise men of Khorassán was the Imám Mowaffak of Naishápúr, a man highly honoured and reverenced ~ may God rejoice his soul; his illustrious years exceeded eighty-five, and it was the universal belief that every boy who read the Koran or studied the traditions in his presence, would assuredly attain to honour and happiness. For this cause did my father send me from Tús to Naishápúr with Abd-u-samad, the doctor of law, that I might employ myself in study and learning under the guidance of that illustrious teacher. Towards me he ever turned an eye of favour and kindness, and as his pupil I felt for him extreme affection and devotion, so that I passed four years in his service. When I first came there, I found two other pupils of mine own age newly arrived, Hakim Omar Khayyám, and the ill-fated Ben Sabbáh. Both were endowed with sharpness of wit and the highest natural powers; and we three formed a close friendship together. When the Imám rose from his lectures, they used to join me, and we repeated to each other the lessons we had heard. Now Omar was a native of Naishápúr, while Hasan Ben Sabbáh's father was one Ali, a man of austere life and practice, but heretical in his creed and doctrine. One day Hasan said to me and to Khayyám, 'It is a universal belief that the pupils of the Imám Mowaffak will attain to fortune. Now, even if we all do not attain thereto, without doubt one of us will; what then shall be our mutual pledge and bond?' We answered, 'Be it what you please.'

'Well', he said, 'let us make a vow, that to whomsoever this fortune falls, he shall share it equally with the rest, and reserve no pre-eminence for himself.' 'Be it so,' we both replied, and on these terms we mutually pledged our words. Years rolled on, and I went from Khorassán to Transoxiana, and wandered to Ghazni and Cabul; and when I returned, I was invested with office, and rose to be administrator of affairs during the Sultanate of Sultan Alp Arslán."

'He goes on to state, that years passed by, and both his old school-friends found him out and came and claimed a share in his good fortune, according to the school-day vow. The Vizier was generous and kept his word. Hasan demanded a place in the government, which the Sultan granted at the Vizier's request; but discontented with a gradual rise, he plunged into the maze of intrigue of an oriental court, and, failing in a base attempt to supplant his benefactor, he was disgraced and fell. After many mishaps and wanderings, Hasan became the head of the Persian sect of the *Ismailians,—* a party of fanatics who had long murmured in obscurity, but rose to an evil eminence under the guidance of his strong and evil will. In A.D. 1090, he seized the castle of Alamút, in the province of Rúdbar, which lies in the mountainous tract south of the Caspian Sea; and it was from this mountain home he obtained that evil celebrity among the Crusaders as the OLD MAN OF THE MOUNTAINS, and spread terror through the Mohammedan world; and it is yet disputed whether the word *Assassin*, which they have left in the language of modern Europe as their dark memorial, is derived from the *hashish*, or opiate of hemp-leaves (the Indian *bhang*), with which they maddened themselves to the sullen pitch of oriental desperation, or from the name of the founder of the dynasty, whom we have seen in his quiet collegiate days, at Naishápúr. One of the countless victims of the Assassin's dagger was Nizám ul Mulk himself, the old school-boy friend.

'Omar Khayyám also came to the Vizier to claim his share; but not to ask for title or office. "The greatest boon you can confer on me," he said, "is to let me live in a corner under the shadow of your fortune, to spread wide the advantages of Science, and pray for your long life and prosperity." The Vizier tells us, that, when he found Omar was really sincere in his refusal, he pressed him no further, but granted him a yearly pension of 1,200 *mithkáls* of gold, from the treasury of Naishápúr.

'At Naishápúr thus lived and died Omar Khayyám, "busied", adds the Vizier, "in winning knowledge of every kind, and especially in Astronomy, wherein he attained to a very high pre-eminence. Under the Sultanate of Malik Shah, he came to Merv, and obtained great praise for his proficiency in science, and the Sultan showered favours upon him."

'When Malik Shah determined to reform the calendar, Omar was one of the eight learned men employed to do it; the result was the *Jaláli* era (so called from *Jalál-ud-din*, one of the king's names)—"a computation of time," says Gibbon, "which surpasses the Julian, and approaches the accuracy of the Gregorian style." He is also the author of some astronomical tables, entitled *Ziji-Malik-sháhi*, and the French have lately republished and translated an Arabic Treatise of his on Algebra.

'These severer Studies, and his Verses, which, though happily fewer than any Persian Poet's, and, though perhaps fugitively composed, the Result of no fugitive Emotion or Thought, are probably the Work and Event of his Life, leaving little else to record. Perhaps he liked a little Farming too, so often as he speaks of the "Edge of the Tilth" on which he loved to rest with his Diwán of Verse, his Loaf ~ and his Wine...

Excerpt from Edward FitzGerald's preface to the First Edition 1859

Those who trace the poems to
their source, and compare
FitzGerald's translation with the
original, are destined both to
disappointment and amazement.
In the Persian, the thought seems
trite and commonplace, the quality
sensual, and even gross. In translation,
it has indeed, like the bones of the
drowned king in The Tempest,
suffered a change 'into something
rich and strange.' The profound
emotion, the wistful melancholy,
the exquisite beauty of form and
cadence are all the added gift of
FitzGerald.

In his hands the spirit of the book is only comparable to the spirit of the Ecclesiastes... He has enriched a bare and simple theme by sweet and solemn harmonies of subtle thought and moving eloquence. As he wrote himself of the book in memorable words, 'It is a desperate sort of thing, unfortunately at the bottom of all thinking men's minds; but made Music of.'

It may be said, to translate that fine sentence into a more harsh and exact terminology, that the poem is perhaps the most stately

and mournful presentation ever
made of Agnosticism, together with
its resultant Epicureanism. It is
the cry of a spirit at bay, confronted
at the same time with the rich and
varied delights of life, the brevity of
all sweet experience, and the terror
of the unknown darkness which
waits to receive the perceptive spirit.
The soul asks itself what the meaning
of it all is. It finds itself in a world
full of beauty and delight, thrilled
with every kind of desirable sensation;
after the first child-like ecstasy is
over, it begins to perceive woven into
the texture, the dark lines of sin and
suffering, of shame and grief, which

transform what might be tranquil
and beautiful into something
harsh and unbearable; and then too
there opens a still darker and mistier
prospect upon the view. Whichever
way it looks, death closes the prospect
like a wall, till the spirit, disillusioned
and terrified, asks itself why it was
placed in so congenial a sphere and
with so immortal an outlook, only
to be confronted with the blank
mystery of extinction.

The only answer to such questionings
is the answer of faith, and that,
to the distracted and melancholy
mind, is nothing more than a

faint hope, a light of sunrise seen across dark valleys and cold mountain ranges.

The greater part of an Introduction written by A.C. Benson, Fellow of Magdalene College, Cambridge. Reproduced from a Manuscript written and illuminated by F. Sangorsky and G. Sutcliffe – 1910.

'When the sinner shall rise from his grave, there shall meet him an uglier figure than ever he beheld—deformed, hideous, of a filthy smell, and with a horrid voice; so that he shall call aloud "God save me! What art thou?" The shape shall answer, "Why wonderest thou at me? I am but Thine Own Works; thou didst ride upon me in the other world, and I will ride upon thee for ever here."'

Jalālu'd~Dīn

A quotation found in the book 'Polonius' written by Edward FitzGerald~1852

'... I was sitting at breakfast alone, & reading some of Moore's Songs: and thinking to myself how it was fame enough to have written but one song-air, or words-which shd in after days solace the Sailor at the wheel, or the Soldier in foreign places!-be taken up into the life of England!...'

Edward FitzGerald~1851
From a letter to Mrs. Cowell

'2nd September, 1863

My dear and very dear Sir,

I do not know in the least who you
are, but I do with all my soul pray
you to find and translate some
more of Omar Khayyám for us:
I never did~till this day~read
anything so glorious, to my mind
as this poem~(10th, 11th, 12th pages
if one were to choose)~and that &
this, is all I can say about it.~More~
more~please more~and I am ever
gratefully and respectfully yours.'

J. Ruskin.

The Translator of the Rubáiyát of Omar.

'FitzGerald is to be called "translator" only in default of a better word, one which should express the poetic transfusion of a poetic spirit from one language to another, and the re-presentation of the ideas and images of the original in a form not altogether diverse from their own, but perfectly adapted to the new conditions of time, place, custom, and habit of mind in which they re-appear. It has all the merit of a remarkable original production, and its excellence is the highest testimony that could be given to the essential impressiveness and

worth of the Persian poet. It is the
work of a poet inspired by the work
of a poet; not a copy, but a reproduction;
not a translation, but the re-delivery
of a poetic inspiration…in its English
dress it reads like the latest and
freshest expression of the perplexity
and of the doubt of the generation
to which we ourselves belong. There
is probably nothing in the mass
of English translations or reproductions
of the poetry of the East to be compared
with this little volume in point of
value as *English* poetry. In the
strength of rhythmical structure, in
force of expression, in musical

modulation, and in mastery of language, the external character of the verse corresponds with the still rarer interior qualities of imagination and of spiritual disernment which it displays.'

A review by Professor C.E. Norton of Harvard University 1870

'It is written in the chronicles of the ancients that this King of the Wise, Omar Khayyám, died at Naishápúr in the year of the Hegira 517 (A.D. 1123); in science he was unrivalled~the very paragon of his age. Khwájah Nizámi of Samarcand, who was one of his pupils, relates the following story:"I often used to hold conversations with my teacher, Omar Khayyám, in a garden; and one day he said to me, 'my tomb shall be in a spot, where the north wind may scatter roses over it.' I wondered at the words he spake, but I knew that his were no idle words. Years after, when I chanced to revisit Naishápúr, I went to his final resting place, and lo! it was just outside a garden, and trees laden with fruit stretched their boughs over the garden wall, and dropped their flowers upon his tomb, so as the stone was hidden under them."'

The *Calcutta Review*
No. LIX from Mirkhond's
'History of the Assassins'

As quoted by Edward
FitzGerald in his preface
to the First Edition 1859

In the year 1893 cuttings from these same roses were planted at the head of Edward FitzGerald's grave in Boulge. Described as 'pink, but not the pink of an English Wild-Rose,' scented with an 'exquisite and subtle' scent, showing small thorns among leaves of a 'beautiful lettuce green,' we may think about those blossoms showering both graves.

'And look—a thousand Blossoms with the Day Woke—and a thousand scatter'd into Clay:'

Condensed from an introduction by Charles Ganz to the Golden Cockerel Press Edition of 1938

I

AWAKE! for Morning in the Bowl of Night
Has flung the Stone that puts the Stars to Flight:
   And Lo! the Hunter of the East has caught
The Sultan's Turret in a Noose of Light.

II

Dreaming when Dawn's Left Hand was in the Sky,
I heard a Voice within the Tavern cry,
    "Awake, my Little Ones, and fill the Cup
Before Life's Liquor in its Cup be dry."

III

And as the Cock crew, those who stood before
The Tavern shouted – "Open then the Door!
    You know how little while we have to stay,
And once departed, may return no more."

IV

Now the New Year reviving old Desires,
The thoughtful Soul to Solitude retires,
　　Where the WHITE HAND of MOSES on the Bough
Puts out, and Jesus from the Ground suspires.

V

Irám indeed is gone with all its Rose,
And Jamshýd's Sev'n-ring'd Cup where no one
　　　　　knows;
　　But still the Vine her ancient Ruby yields,
And still a Garden by the Water blows.

VI

And David's Lips are lock't; but in divine
High-piping Péhlevi, with "Wine! Wine! Wine!
  Red Wine!"—the Nightingale cries to the Rose
That yellow Cheek of hers t'incarnadine.

VII

Come, fill the Cup, and in the Fire of Spring
Your Winter Garment of Repentance fling:
  The Bird of Time has but a little way
To fly—and Lo! the Bird is on the Wing.

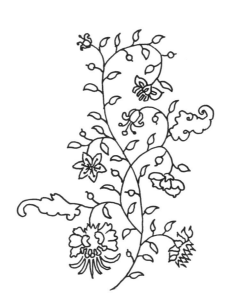

VIII

And look - a thousand Blossoms with the Day
Woke - and a thousand scatter'd into Clay:
    And this first Summer Month that brings
        the Rose
Shall take Jamshýd and Kaikobád away.

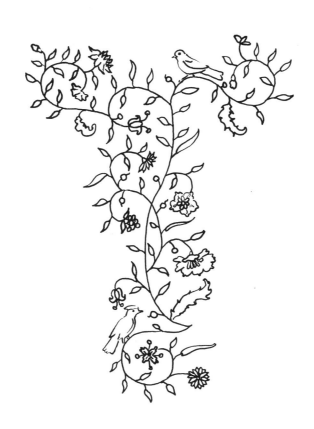

IX

But come with old Khayyám and leave the Lot
Of Kaikobád and Kaikhosrú forgot:
    Let Rustum lay about him as he will,
Or Hátim Tai cry Supper—heed them not.

X

With me along some strip of Herbage strown
That just divides the desert from the sown,
    Where name of Slave and Sultán scarce
        is known,
And pity Sultán Máhmúd on his Throne.

XI

Here with a Loaf of Bread beneath the Bough,
A Jug of Wine, a Book of Verse – and Thou
  Beside me singing in the Wilderness –
Oh, Wilderness were Paradise enow!

XII

Some for the Glories of This World; and some
Sigh for the Prophet's Paradise to come;
    Ah, take the Cash, and let the Credit go,
Nor heed the rumble of a distant Drum!

XIII

Look to the blowing Rose about us—"Lo,
Laughing," she says, "into the World I blow:
    At once the silken Tassel of my Purse
Tear, and its Treasure on the Garden throw.

XIV

The Worldly Hope men set their Hearts upon
Turns Ashes – or it prospers; and anon,
　　Like Snow upon the Desert's dusty Face
Lighting a little Hour or two – is gone.

XV

And those who husbanded the Golden Grain,
And those who flung it to the Winds like Rain,
　　Alike to no such aureate Earth are turn'd
As, buried once, Men want dug up again.

XVI

Think, in this battered Caravanserai
Whose Doorways are alternate Night and Day,
    How Sultán after Sultán with his Pomp
Abode his Hour or two, and went his way.

XVII

They say the Lion and the Lizard keep
The Courts where Jamshyd gloried and drank deep:
    And Bahrám, that great Hunter—the Wild Ass
Stamps o'er his Head, but cannot break his Sleep.

XVIII

The Palace that to Heav'n his pillars threw,
And Kings the forehead on his threshold drew—
    I saw the solitary Ringdove there,
And "Coo, coo, coo," she cried; and "Coo, coo, coo."

XIX

I sometimes think that never blows so red
The Rose as where some buried Caesar bled;
    That every Hyacinth the Garden wears
Dropt in her Lap from some once lovely Head.

XX

And this delightful Herb whose tender Green
Fledges the River's Lip on which we lean~
    Ah, lean upon it lightly! for who knows
From what once Lovely Lip it springs unseen!

XXI

Ah, my Belovéd, fill the Cup that clears
TO-DAY of past Regrets and future Fears~
    To-morrow ?~Why, To-morrow I may be
Myself with Yesterday's Sev'n Thousand Years.

XXII

Lo! some we loved, the loveliest and best
That Time and Fate of all their Vintage prest,
    Have drunk their Cup a Round or two before,
And one by one crept silently to Rest.

XXIII

And we, that now make merry in the Room
They left, and Summer dresses in new bloom,
    Ourselves must we beneath the Couch of Earth
Descend, ourselves to make a Couch~for whom?

XXIV

Ah, make the most of what we yet may spend,
Before we too into the Dust descend;
    Dust into Dust, and under Dust, to lie,
Sans Wine, sans Song, sans Singer, and~sans End!

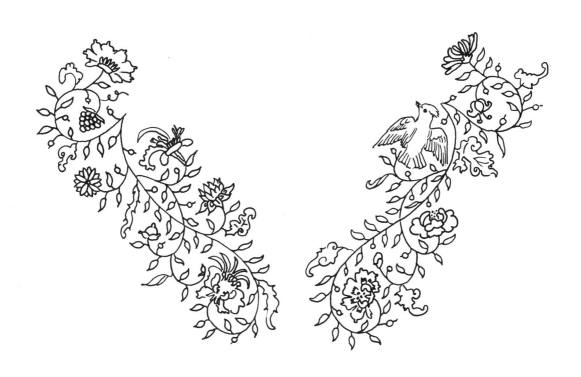

XXV

Alike for those who for TO-DAY prepare,
And those that after some TO-MORROW stare,
   A Muezzin from the Tower of Darkness cries,
"Fools! your Reward is neither Here nor There!"

XXVI

Why, all the Saints and Sages who discuss'd
Of the Two Worlds so learnedly, are thrust
    Like foolish Prophets forth; their Words to scorn
Are scatter'd, and their Mouths are stopt with Dust.

XXVII

Myself when young did eagerly frequent
Doctor and Saint, and heard great Argument
    About it and about: but evermore
Came out by the same Door where in I went.

XXVIII

With them the Seed of Wisdom did I sow,
And with mine own hand labour'd it to grow:
    And this was all the Harvest that I reap'd—
"I came like Water, and like Wind I go."

XXIX

Into this Universe, and *why* not knowing,
Nor *whence*, like Water willy-nilly flowing;
    And out of it, as Wind along the Waste,
I know not *whither*, willy-nilly blowing.

XXX

What, without asking, hither hurried *whence*?
And, without asking, *whither* hurried hence!
    Oh, many a Cup of this forbidden Wine
Must drown the memory of that insolence!

XXXI

Up from Earth's Centre through the Seventh Gate
I rose, and on the Throne of Saturn sate,
   And many a Knot unravel'd by the Road;
But not the Knot of Human Death and Fate.

XXXII

There was a Door to which I found no Key:
There was a Veil past which I could not see:
   Some little Talk awhile of ME and THEE
There seemed—and then no more of THEE and ME.

XXXIII

Earth could not answer; nor the Seas that mourn
In flowing Purple, of their Lord forlorn;
    Nor rolling Heaven, with all his Signs reveal'd
And hidden by the sleeve of Night and Morn.

XXXIV

Then to the rolling Heav'n itself I cried,
Asking, "What Lamp had Destiny to guide
   Her little Children stumbling in the Dark?"
And—"A blind Understanding!" Heav'n replied.

XXXV

Then to this earthen Bowl did I adjourn
My Lip the secret Well of Life to learn:
   And Lip to Lip it murmur'd—"While you live
Drink! for once dead you never shall return."

XXXVI

I think the Vessel, that with fugitive
Articulation answer'd, once did live,
    And drink; and Ah! the passive Lip I kiss'd,
How many Kisses might it take - and give!

XXXVII

For in the Market-place, one Dusk of Day,
I watch'd the Potter thumping his wet Clay:
    And with its all obliterated Tongue
It murmur'd ~ "Gently, Brother, gently, pray!"

XXXVIII

And has not such a Story from of Old
Down Man's successive generations roll'd
    Of such a clod of saturated Earth
Cast by the Maker into Human mould?

XXXIX

And not a drop that from our Cups we throw
For Earth to drink of, but may steal below
  To quench the fire of Anguish in some Eye
There hidden~far beneath, and long ago.

XL

As then the Tulip for her morning sup
Of Heav'nly Vintage from the soil looks up,
  Do you devoutly do the like, till Heav'n
To Earth invert you~like an empty Cup.

XLI

Perplext no more with Human or Divine,
To-morrow's tangle to the winds resign,
  And lose your fingers in the tresses of
The Cypress-slender Minister of Wine.

XLII

And if the Wine you drink, the Lip you press,
End in the Nothing all Things end in~Yes~
   Then fancy while Thou art, Thou art but what
Thou shalt be~Nothing~Thou shalt not be less.

XLIII

While the Rose blows along the River Brink,
With old Khayyám the Ruby Vintage drink:
   And when the Angel with his darker Draught
Draws up to Thee~take that, and do not shrink.

XLIV

Why, if the Soul can fling the Dust aside,
And naked on the Air of Heaven ride,
    Were't not a Shame — were't not a Shame for him
In this clay carcase crippled to abide?

XLV

'Tis but a Tent where takes his one day's rest
A Sultán to the realm of Death addrest;
    The Sultán rises, and the dark Ferrásh
Strikes, and prepares it for another Guest.

XLVI

And fear not lest Existence closing your
Account, and mine, should know the like no more;
    The Eternal Sákí from that Bowl has pour'd
Millions of Bubbles like us, and will pour.

XLVII

When You and I behind the Veil are past,
Oh, but the long, long while the World shall last,
    Which of our Coming and Departure heeds
As the Sev'n Seas should heed a pebble-cast.

XLVIII

One Moment in Annihilation's Waste,
One Moment, of the Well of Life to taste—
    The Stars are setting and the Caravan
Starts for the Dawn of Nothing—Oh, make haste!

XLIX

Would you that spangle of Existence spend
About THE SECRET—quick about it, Friend!
    A Hair perhaps divides the False and True—
And upon what, prithee, may life depend?

L

A Hair perhaps divides the False and True;
Yes; and a single Alif were the clue—
    Could you but find it—to the Treasure-house,
And peradventure to THE MASTER too;

LI

Whose secret Presence, through Creation's veins
Running Quicksilver-like eludes your pains;
    Taking all shapes from Máh to Máhi; and
They change and perish all—but He remains;

LII

A moment guess'd– then back behind the Fold
Immerst of Darkness round the Drama roll'd
   Which, for the Pastime of Eternity,
He doth Himself contrive, enact, behold.

LIII

How long, how long, in infinite Pursuit
Of This and That endeavor and dispute?
   Better be merry with the fruitful Grape
Than sadden after none, or bitter, Fruit.

LIV

You know, my Friends, how long since in my House
For a new Marriage I did make Carouse:
    Divorced old barren Reason from my Bed,
And took the Daughter of the Vine to Spouse.

LV

For "IS" and "IS-NOT" though *with* Rule and Line,
And "UP-AND-DOWN" *without*, I could define,
    I yet in all I only cared to know,
Was never deep in anything but–Wine.

LVI

Ah, fill the Cup:– what boots it to repeat
How time is slipping underneath our Feet:
    Unborn TO-MORROW and dead YESTERDAY,
Why fret about them if TO-DAY be sweet!

LVII

And lately, by the Tavern Door agape,
Came shining through the Dusk an Angel Shape
    Bearing a Vessel on his Shoulder; and
He bid me taste of it; and 'twas – the Grape!

LVIII

The Grape that can with Logic absolute
The Two-and-Seventy jarring Sects confute:
    The sovereign Alchemist that in a Trice
Life's leaden Metal into Gold transmute.

LIX

The mighty Mahmúd, the victorious Lord
That all the misbelieving and black Horde
    Of Fears and Sorrows that infest the Soul
Scatters and slays with his enchanted Sword.

LX

Why, be this Juice the growth of God, who dare
Blaspheme the twisted tendril as a Snare?
    A Blessing, we should use it, should we not?
And if a Curse ~ why, then, Who set it there?

LXI

I must abjure the Balm of Life, I must,
Scared by some After-reckoning ta'en on trust,
    Or lured with Hope of some Diviner Drink,
To fill the Cup ~ when crumbled into Dust!

LXII

Oh, threats of Hell and Hopes of Paradise!
One thing at least is certain—*This* Life flies,
　　One thing is certain and the rest is Lies;
The Flower that once has blown for ever dies.

LXIII

Strange, is it not? that of the myriads who
Before us pass'd the door of Darkness through,
    Not one returns to tell us of the Road,
Which to discover we must travel too.

LXIV

The Revelations of Devout and Learn'd
Who rose before us, and as Prophets burn'd,
    Are all but Stories, which awoke from Sleep
They told their comrades, and to Sleep return'd.

LXV

I sent my Soul through the Invisible,
Some letter of that After-life to spell:
    And by and by my Soul return'd to me,
And answer'd "I Myself am Heav'n and Hell:"

LXVI

Heav'n but the Vision of fulfill'd Desire,
And Hell the Shadow from a Soul on fire,
    Cast on the Darkness into which Ourselves,
So late emerged from, shall so soon expire.

LXVII

But leave the Wise to wrangle, and with me
The Quarrel of the Universe let be:
    And, in some corner of the Hubbub coucht,
Make Game of that which makes as much of Thee.

LXVIII

For in and out, above, about, below,
'Tis nothing but a Magic Shadow-show,
    Play'd in a Box whose Candle is the Sun,
Round which we Phantom Figures come and go.

LXIX

'Tis all a Chequer-board of Nights and Days
Where Destiny with Men for Pieces plays:
    Hither and thither moves, and mates, and slays,
And one by one back in the Closet lays.

LXX

The Ball no Question makes of Ayes and Noes,
But Here or There as strikes the Player goes;
    And He that toss'd Thee down into the Field,
He knows about it all~ He knows~ HE knows!

LXXI

The Moving Finger writes; and, having writ,
Moves on: nor all thy Piety nor Wit
    Shall lure it back to cancel half a Line,
Nor all thy Tears wash out a Word of it.

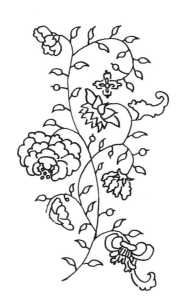

LXXII

For let Philosopher and Doctor preach
Of what they will, and what they will not~each
    Is but one Link in an eternal Chain
That none can slip, nor break, nor over~reach.

LXXIII

And that inverted Bowl we call the Sky,
Whereunder crawling coop'd we live and die,
    Lift not thy hands to *It* for help~for It
As impotently rolls as Thou or I.

LXXIV

With Earth's first Clay They did the Last Man knead,
And then of the Last Harvest sow'd the Seed:
    Yea, the first Morning of Creation wrote
What the Last Dawn of Reckoning shall read.

LXXV

YESTERDAY *This* Day's Madness did prepare;
TO-MORROW'S Silence, Triumph, or Despair:
    Drink! for you know not whence you came,
        nor why:
Drink! for you know not why you go, nor where.

LXXVI

I tell Thee this - When, started from the Goal,
Over the flaming shoulders of the Foal
    Of Heav'n Parwín and Mushtarí they flung,
In my predestin'd Plot of Dust and Soul

LXXVII

The Vine had struck a Fibre; which about
If clings my Being - let the Súfi flout;
    Of my Base Metal may be filed a Key,
That shall unlock the Door he howls without.

LXXVIII

And this I know: whether the one True Light
Kindle to Love, or Wrath - consume me quite,
    One Glimpse of It within the Tavern caught
Better than in the Temple lost outright.

LXXIX

Oh Thou, who didst with Pitfall and with Gin
Beset the Road I was to wander in,
    Thou wilt not with Predestination round
Enmesh me, and impute my Fall to Sin?

LXXX

Oh Thou, who Man of baser Earth didst make,
And who with Eden didst devise the Snake;
    For all the Sin wherewith the Face of man
Is blacken'd-Man's Forgiveness give-and take!

KÚZA-NÁMA

LXXXI

Listen again. One evening at the Close
Of Ramazán, ere the better Moon arose,
    In that old Potter's Shop I stood alone
With the clay Population round in Rows.

LXXXII

And, strange to tell, among that Earthen Lot
Some could articulate, while others not:
    And suddenly one more impatient cried—
"Who *is* the Potter, pray, and who the Pot?"

LXXXIII

Said one among them—"Surely not in vain
My substance from the common Earth was ta'en;
 That He who subtly wrought me into Shape
Should stamp me back to common Earth again."

LXXXIV

Then said a Second—"Ne'er a peevish Boy
Would break the Bowl from which he drank in Joy;
 And He that with His hand the Vessel made
Will surely not in after Wrath destroy."

LXXXV

None answered this; but after Silence spake
A Vessel of a more ungainly Make:
    "They sneer at me for leaning all awry;
What! did the Hand then of the Potter shake?"

LXXXVI

"Why," said another, "Some there are who tell
Of one who threatens he will toss to Hell
    The luckless Pots he marr'd in making-Pish!
He's a Good Fellow, and 'twill all be well."

LXXXVII

"Well," murmur'd one, "Let whoso make or buy,
My Clay with long Oblivion is gone dry:
    But, fill me with the old familiar Juice,
Methinks I might recover by and by."

LXXXVIII

So while the Vessels one by one were speaking,
One spied the little Crescent all were seeking:
    And then they jogged each other, "Brother!
        Brother!
Hark to the Porter's Shoulder-knot a-creaking!"

LXXXIX

Ah, with the Grape my fading Life provide,
And wash my Body whence the Life has died,
　　And in a Winding-sheet of Vine-leaf wrapt,
So bury me by some sweet Garden-side.

XC

That ev'n my buried Ashes such a Snare
Of Vintage shall fling up into the Air,
　　As not a True Believer passing by
But shall be overtaken unaware.

XCI

Indeed the Idols I have loved so long
Have done my Credit in this World much wrong,
   Have drowned my Honour in a shallow Cup,
And sold my Reputation for a Song.

XCII

Indeed, indeed, Repentance oft before
I swore ~ but was I sober when I swore?
   And then and then came Spring, and Rose-in-
        hand
My thread-bare Penitence apieces tore.

XCIII

And much as Wine has played the Infidel,
And robb'd me of my Robe of Honour—well,
  I wonder often what the Vintners buy
One half so precious as the Goods they sell.

XCIV

Alas, that Spring should vanish with the Rose!
That Youth's sweet-scented Manuscript should
        close!
  The Nightingale that in the Branches sang,
Ah, whence, and whither flown again, who knows?

XCV

Oh if the World were but to re-create,
That we might catch ere closed the Book of Fate,
    And make The Writer on a fairer leaf
Inscribe our names, or quite obliterate!

XCVI

Ah, Love, could thou and I with Him conspire
To grasp this sorry Scheme of Things entire,
    Would not we shatter it to bits~and then
Re-mould it nearer to the Heart's Desire!

XCVII

Ah, Moon of my Delight who know'st no wane,
The Moon of Heav'n is rising once again:
   How oft hereafter rising shall she look
Through this same Garden-and for *one* in vain!

XCVIII

And when Thyself with shining Foot shall pass
Among the Guests Star-scattered on the Grass,
   And in thy joyous errand reach the spot
Where I made one-turn down an empty Glass!

TAMÁM SHUD

WHY

I remember the bright green paint, the bustling black taxis, the curious outdoor book stalls. London was magic. London was different. Sun shone in the air. I was seventeen years old in London with my younger sister and cousin, exhilarating in my first grown-up adventure away from home.

'Well, girls, what can we do for you this fine morning?'

Mr. Joseph's gruff voice welcomed us to E. Joseph of Charing Cross Road. Mr. Joseph's penetrating eyes had the the funniest way of selling books. We were sure he liked us, because he allowed us an hour in his cellar and another hour in his musty back room. We knew we were seeing treasures.

'This is my gold girls. Take a good look. You won't see gold like this every day.'

How proud he was - old Mr. Joseph - of the world he had collected in those few rooms.

Who could resist his insidious voice with its kindly knowledge of teenage poverty, its sure instinct that we could afford nothing. We would show him. We bought - hesitantly at first - a few glorious volumes each. I still have mine - 22 years older - one of them slim and green, covered in something exotic he called 'Morocco'. It travelled with me through England, Scotland, and Wales. Through all the homely bread and breakfast places - the quaint charm - the welcoming welcomes. The fragrant smell of old leather permeated my suitcase.

At night, just before falling asleep, I would secretly open its covers. *The Rubáiyát of Omar Khayyám*. How mysterious. How tantalizing. What was Rubáiyát and Omar and Khayyám? What was this lovely strange land? How it peopled my dreams with half understood phrases:

'Dreaming when Dawn's Left Hand was in the Sky,
I heard a Voice within the Tavern cry,...'

For me that summer would always be woven through my memory with a thread called Rubáiyát. It would always be linked to the man I married - a tall, thin Scotsman - who - when he marched the moors with steady step swinging his dark green kilt - I knew to be as romantic, as far removed from my world, as my already incomparable Rubáiyát.

I never told him I was afraid of the night though, afraid of the silent monsters howling in the dark. I never told him I was afraid to die. Tossing and turning, continually needing a light. Where would I go and why and how would I answer the questions when I got there?

After a few years, I didn't need to tell him. My book was telling me. Edward FitzGerald and Omar Khayyám. They were teaching me acceptance. I accept. This strange kind of poetry inspired answers to my anxious questions. I became more at one with the trees and the flowers, the continuity of living. I stopped being afraid to die.

Years passed. One winter I caught pneumonia. Relentlessly it pursued me until that first perfect day of getting well. It was so luxurious to lie in bed and not hurt anywhere. My hands seemed transparent - alien - were they really me? Was I really in Canada? The snow slowly drifting down, the great Saskatchewan River frozen and white. I wasn't allowed out of bed; I had promised. I lay awhile, idly at peace, listening to the far away shrieks of babies and puppies and a pet otter tumbling in the soft snow. I began to feel so well that I thought,

> 'Remember those new books we bought last year in England? I'll just take a peek.'

One title stood out from the rest. Why, *The Rubáiyát of Omar Khayyám*! It had a different binding, different illustrations. A perfect get-well book with a gold peacock spreading its tail across the cover. The manuscript writing glowed like a jewel. Goodness! Close by I saw another Rubáiyát. Why here were still more Rubáiyáts, all together on one bookshelf. I was thrilled. Riches of Rubáiyáts. My husband must have bought them to surprise me. He had succeeded.

> 'Hey, wait a minute - they made a mistake here. This isn't the Rubáiyát.'

I was cross. I felt disturbed. How could they so carelessly make mistakes in books like these, all leather and gold with hand-made, crinkle-edged paper. I kept on reading. I began to agonize. So many of my incomparable verses had changed. Their dreamlike drifting beauty seemed dulled and tarnished. WHAT HAD HAPPENED? Who could dare change verses no genius could improve? FitzGerald would be furious. And then - what was this verse here? What was this whole group of verses? They weren't in my book. Somebody *had* made a mistake!

I read the introduction by Arthur Christopher Benson. I snatched up my faithful companion of the years, and began frantically to compare...

'What is going on here? Why aren't you still in bed?' A fierce voice broke through my frenzy.

'Oh, Sandy, Sandy, my book isn't alone. It doesn't stand alone. He wrote it again and again. How could he? I hate him. He changed my beautiful verses.'

I burst into tears.

• • • •

Slowly, in the days which followed this misery, my strength began to return, but not my happiness. No. I felt bitter and betrayed. Somebody had hurt me. Somebody had done it on purpose. Not a "Song of Songs", not an "Ecclesiastes", only a collection of Editions. Edition I, Edition II, Edition III, Edition IV, Edition V. I was bewildered, dissatisfied. He could keep his old books. I certainly wasn't going to read any of them again. A lot I cared.

Time passed, soothing my bruises, making me stronger.

'Why not? Why don't you read all those editions just once? Why don't you give them a try? Maybe you'll be surprised. Maybe FitzGerald had to keep writing. Maybe he couldn't help it.'

Finally I acquiesced to that insistent voice. At least I would read the Second Edition, having by now discovered that my own gem was the First Edition. Ghastly. These verses were worse than ever. FitzGerald must have had a headache. He couldn't have written them. He never would have tolerated such awkward phrasing. But oh the Dulacs! Edmund Dulac, my childhood favorite artist. And was this a new verse— a verse I had never seen before? Could this be another? Quickly I checked the four remaining editions. But these were exquisite. Why did he leave them out of III, out of IV, out of V? Why were they only in II?

'Come on Cecile, be reasonable. Now that you've read the Second Edition, how about trying the Third, the Fourth, and the Fifth? Maybe there are more verses to rejoice the heart. Who knows? A sunbeam here and a sunbeam there. Don't stop now. Quick. Open those other books.'

I listened. Part of me listened. The other part ached.

'Awake! for Morning in the Bowl of Night
Has flung the Stone that puts the Stars to Flight:'

Murdered, dead, gone, killed. How could anybody throw away that verse? Who could justify such an action?

Finally from those days of turmoil began to grow a small flower of thought.

WHAT IF?

What if someone compared the Five FitzGerald Editions choosing only *their* idea of the best rhythms, the loveliest images, the deepest meaning, limiting their quest to FitzGerald himself, using only *his* verses, *his* words, and *his* punctuation?

With which of these three lines should this verse begin?

I.XI'Here with a Loaf of Bread beneath the Bough,'

II.XII'Here with a little Bread beneath the Bough,'

III, IV, V.XII'A Book of Verses underneath the Bough,'

How should this same verse end?

I.XI 'And Wilderness is Paradise enow.'

II, III, IV, V. XII 'Oh, Wilderness were Paradise enow!'

But me? I wasn't a poet, not even a writer, not even a scholar.

'But you care Cécile. Try it. Just try it. When? When could I ever? Oh I couldn't. I really couldn't.'

One little baby still at home, two in school, the day so full of trying to be a wife, a mother. How about early in the morning? That was an idea.

So for a year, for two years, early in the cold and dark of winter, I would creep downstairs to sit curled up beside our Buddha lamps, copying out in green and black, in red and purple and orange, all the five editions. During the rest of the day I was cross and horrid. I was short of sleep and nobody liked me. I wasn't oblivious to the wrong I was doing my family, but I needed to see my Rubáiyát grow. It became a passion. I would puzzle and ponder and ask the laughing baby whether he preferred, 'yellow Cheek t'incarnadine' or 'sallow cheek to incarnadine.'

More years passed. More cubbyholes of time. I stole them from life here and then from life there. Hawksbill Cay in the West Indies. Alone in a sea-wilderness listening to the Osprey's mournful cry. I would bask in the hot afternoon sun, watch the fish leaping silver in its light, and ask myself again and again which and how. I would write and rewrite, still with five colored pens. The book was taking so long put together in these hopscotch squares of time, I was growing frustrated. If I could just have a whole year off, instead of filling up my few precious freedoms now bursting with new ideas. Wearily I started dating decisions.

CEM 1971.

CEM 1973.

A flower in the margin meant I wasn't sure. The flowers would diminish one year, proliferate the next. Despair engulfed me. When would I ever know?

Since the answer was obviously 'never', I decided at least to begin my introduction. Six months of work later, with a feeling of satisfied pleasure, I read it aloud to my assembled family. In the long silence which followed, I was distressingly aware of kind-hearted, horror-filled faces.

'Could you try it again Mummy?'

This from my tactful eldest concerned for the family honour.

My grown-up six year old patted me generously.

'It'll be easier next time Mummy. You'll see. Don't cry.'

'You wouldn't want us to lie would you Mummy?'

As usual Fiona's blue eyes pierced the heart.

No. No lies thank you. I put it away in a drawer. It could stay there forever.

And then I read Christopher Ricks' 'Collection of Poems by Alfred Tennyson'. The people of his foreword lived on high mountain tops. Ricks allowed *their* voices to speak *his* ideas. I would copy him, rationalizing about beginners being allowed to steal. If only he could guess my gratitude.

My second introduction was 100 pages long with stars shining through. Finally it was reduced to just the stars.

Next came decisions about illustrations. I loved Dulac, but sometimes I preferred the Pogány of my first little, green Morocco volume. How to copy these pictures without turning the yellows to green, the blues to purple. All modern books seemed unable to reproduce the beautiful color nuances of older Dulac illustrations. Why? How would I succeed where they had failed?

I decided to visit the publisher Harrap. Although long familiarity had bred my great admiration for Pogány's bittersweet illustrations even one so infatuated as myself had to admit that the only reproductions in my possession lacked quality. If there existed clearer duplicates, my most diligent search had so far failed to locate them.

The kindest man in a big round office high above busy London streets calmly smoked a cigar and said in a genial voice,

'Well, Mrs. Mactaggart, I wish I could help you find the originals. They used to hang all around the walls of this office. I remember Pogány well.'

I waited, expectant.

'I'm sorry. The war you know. They were bombed out during the war. Not a stone was left. If I had them you would be welcome Mrs. Mactaggart, very welcome indeed, but you see, I don't.'

I departed, reflective about war. I already knew I had to find the originals. The New York Metropolitan Museum had generously recommended me to their engraver a long time ago.

'Well, unless you have the original, you first of all make a copper plate.'

'How much does a copper plate cost?'

'$30,000.'

'$30,000 for one picture?' I gasped. I needed ten.

'Why can't you photocopy these pictures instead of using a copper plate?'

My reasonable question was answered with a lot of incomprehensible technicalities. The one gleam of light I could understand was that my pictures were made up of little squares invisible to the human eye, and original pictures were solid with no little squares. Little squares cost money and no little squares were cheap.

'So that's it. That's why Macmillan and Garden City have greens instead of yellows and purples instead of blues. Got it?' demanded the printer man.

I got the $30,000 alright.

Maybe I should pursue Dulac.

"Yes, I knew Edmund Dulac well. We used to show his paintings at our Leicester Galleries.' Mr. Brown was very helpful.

'I am sure the ones you're after were sold at Sotheby's in 1918.'

Sotheby's on the telephone:

'Quite right, Madam, we did sell those paintings. Records? I am sorry Madam, our records were bombed out during the war. No one could tell you who bought those paintings now.'

Stymied.

In 1975 my husband decided that for too much of our married life he had been a very busy business man, and that if he was ever to know his children before they grew into adults, now was the time. It seemed he could best accomplish this admirable end by buying a sailboat and cruising with us all to the remoter areas of the South Pacific.

I doubt if I will ever forget that voyage. Either I was terrified or seasick or both. I remember laying out pages all over the upper deckhouse while muttering darkly.

'I'll have a picture here. Now I'll have another picture here. My book is going to be different. In my book, pictures are going to be opposite the poems they represent.'

'Mummy, why do they make books and you have to turn the pages so far to find the right picture?'

I could remember that three-year-old voice from the long ago days when we lived on dry land. My book wasn't going to disappoint little children.

'Stupid. Cécile, why are you laying out these pictures? Who's going to spend $30,000 on one picture, and who likes green suns and purple skies? Who's going to read your book anyway?'

I pondered this serious question while throwing up over the side. Seeking solace afterwards, I looked above at the huge sails billowing in, billowing out. This was worse than the 'Ancient Mariner.' Where was the wind? I wished I were dead. Roll on one side. Roll to the other. I hated boats.

Grimly I returned to the deckhouse and carefully placed on the floor all of my poems and all of my pictures, side by side. Luncheon was served. I was oblivious. I was going to finish my book or die. First an enormous roll, then an enormous crash, and finally hot tomato soup all over the white carpet, all over the poems, all over the pictures of the only copy I had on board. Tomato soup glue. Scared little eyes peered out of the silence. He wailed,

'But Mummy. I couldn't help it. The boat almost rolled over.'

We hugged each other. Right then we both hated boats.

LAND HO! The Marquesas and giant, green jade grapefruit. Give up. The book would never be finished. We would probably sink in a typhoon anyway.

By 1976, however, I was still alive and allowed to celebrate this fact by a brief visit to London. I met Mr. Harley and his Curwen Press.

'But Mrs. Mactaggart, you don't need those plates. Not now. Time has passed. Today you don't need originals. Today things are different. If you like the illustrations in your books, if these satisfy you, we can reproduce them exactly. Maybe we can improve them.'

He followed this mind shattering statement with ten minutes of patient printerese while I nodded my head and beamed. I was ecstatic. Could you believe it? My troubles were over. Now I could have my pictures. Now I was ready to go and visit the British Museum.

I dressed in my most appealing clothes. My heart beat fast.

'Come in Mrs. Mactaggart. Do come in.'

I explained my project.

'Oh, but my dear Mrs. Mactaggart, I am afraid you are wasting your time. So many books on the subject, and there is such a thing as copyright you know.'

'Umm. Could we just look? Please just look. I think I am the first. I really think I am.'

I used all my persuasive arts. I tried to look pretty. Finally the learned gentleman's reserve melted a little, and shaking his head as if he could already guess the futility of such a search, he led the way into a majestic dome-ceilinged room filled with gigantic portfolios. Hours passed. He turned the slow white pages - pages as big as men.

Tension mounted. Suddenly he looked up at me curiously. There was a moment of silence.

'My dear Mrs. Mactaggart.'

Now he frankly beamed. He extended his hand.

'I think you're the first. See - I'm writing your name down here. Now you're protected. It's a sort of copyright.'

My heart sang songs all the way to Sangorsky and Sutcliffe - book-binders. I climbed some stairs. Then some more stairs. A last breathless flight, and I was confronted with another century. A little door. A corridor with dark floorboards curving up and down from time past. Mr. and Mrs. Bray.

Mrs. Bray and cups of tea and Mr. Bray being cross with me, telling me why I couldn't, telling me the cost, telling me I didn't know anything. And Mrs. Bray consoling.

'Well you could have some in canvas. Canvas is very nice dear, not nearly so expensive.'

A few days later my husband tried his luck. My husband is wiser and not so impetuous. Mr. Bray began to relent. Mrs. Bray's eyes began to dance. Mr. Bray decided to show us his wealth. From a nondescript cupboard he carefully lowered a large, white leather book, interlaced all over with tiny gold leaves, each leaf attached to curving gold vines with a tiny gold stem. 5,432 leaves with 5,432 steams all applied by hand. Mr. Bray smiled with extreme satisfaction. I was wistful.

'Could I have a book like that?'

'Yes, you could. IF the man who made it was still alive, if time didn't cost, if people cared, if beauty counted if HURRY wasn't King. IF.'

From silent contemplation of past perfection, we slowly pulled ourselves towards drearier present reality.

'My book?'

Mr. Bray's old irascibility with the continuum of incompetence took charge. I was cowed.

'But Mrs. Mactaggart what *is* all this talk about? Your book. Your book. Your book. You've not even finished your book and you talk about bindings and paper.'

His eyes glared straight through me. He was right!

I hurried away. 'Not even finished yet.' The words echoed dolefully in my brain. This was taking Y E A R S . I hardened my heart. At the next stop I was going to work - work and work no matter what - until it was finished. Hateful old thing.

The boat was scheduled for dry dock, so the next stop was a convent situated high in Hiniduma, a mountain fastness of Sri Lanka.

'You'll like it Cécile,' insisted my beloved as he plopped us all down for a month and flew off to business in Canada. 'You'll like it.'

I loved it. I walked the mountain paths fiercely intoning, 'yellow Cheek t'incarnadine, sallow cheek to incarnadine'.

For breakfast, for lunch, for dinner we ate beguiling foreign food. The nuns were incandescent in their long white robes, always laughing, always giving God their hands to help their fellows. My children helped too. They dug in the garden. They made envelopes from old Christmas Cards for Sister Alexander.

'Let's not leave Mummy, let's not leave.'

'Let's finish my book,' I retorted, relentless. 'Now or never.'

I turned to Alastair. Alastair was seven years old.

'What do you think Alastair? I'll read it to you. Do you like "That yellow Cheek of hers t' incarnadine," or do you like "That sallow cheek of hers to incarnadine".'

His bright eyes snapped.

'First of all what does it mean Mummy? That's the most important. You have to decide what it means. Then you can decide what is best.'

Mara was twelve. She was scornful.

'Any dummy knows that if you put your face near a pink rose, and if the light is coming from a certain direction your face will look pink.'

'What does sallow mean Mummy? I think sallow is too sickly to use. I don't like its sound. Let's not choose sallow.'

This from my middle child—my golden-haired, blue-eyed, dreaming child Fiona.

'OK Mummy I agree. You can talk to us at breakfast, lunch, and dinner. We'll help you out. But. Then for six whole months afterwards, no talk at all.'

'Yes, yes,' chimed in the others. 'Let's finish this dumb book for good Mummy. We're sick of your book. It's getting sickening.'

So we argued. We voted. We shouted at each other. We exclaimed. We pouted when our votes were overridden. I was firm.

'This is a democracy children. In democracies the majority rules.'

The bougainvillæa bloomed - a paean of rejoicing - and the slow bullocks, step by ponderous step, drew their home-made ploughs through wet rice fields. The final day came. The final votes. The impossible choices were made - still impossible. The book was finished. No more second looks, no more reconsidering, no more flowers growing. We did a dance. Hurrah! The nuns wondered if the sun . . . ?

● ● ● ●

'Do you think anyone will ever read this book Mummy?'

Oh question of questions, spilling lead through the hours. For my Mother. Would anyone ever admire her calligraphy? A whole year of her life with her fingers arthritic and her obligations undone, while she wrote and rewrote, and spilled the ink and made mistakes and copied again. Then again.

'But Cécile my drawings are so clumsy.'

'I like them Mummy. I like them.'

A year later - 1977 - we were still on board our boat with the voyage drawing to a close. Alastair was a year older.

'Aren't people starving, Mummy? Why don't you give your money to the starving? How come you're making a book?'

'Best paper, best pictures, best leather. No I won't compromise. I'll give the profits to the World Wildlife Fund.'

I talked to myself as I busily worked away, momentarily ignoring Alastair's pertinent question.

'Profits Cécile?'

Sandy was astonished. He raised his eyebrows at me.

'Who says there are going to be any profits Cécile? What's the World Wildlife Fund going to do then? What are you going to do with 200 books that nobody buys? Do you have 200 friends Cécile? Do you?'

'I can't hear you Sandy - I'm talking to Alastair,' I replied haughtily.

'Well Alastair, it's not money that is going to solve the world's problems darling. It's money and time. But mostly time - personal time. Anyhow this is my hobby. People are allowed to have hobbies on the side. Imagine that I want to give the world a splendid tree. I want my tree to provide shade. I want its beauty to refresh the weary. But I am unable. I am too poor. My talent is not unique. I have no genius. I do not know how to build a tree. Suddenly I see a way of making one leaf. Finally and at last this is me finishing my leaf. Trees need leaves. Understand?'

Alastair looked at me quizzically. Had I persuaded him?

●　　　●　　　●　　　●

The voices in my mind kept on nagging.

'If this is so good, why do you have to publish it yourself Cécile? Why not take it to a publisher and he'll publish it? Millions of copies if it is so good?'

'Well he can if he likes - later. But not now. Not this time. Publishers spoil things. They like to do things their own way. They like to make money. They'll put the pictures on the wrong pages. Presents have to be perfect. They have to be the best.'

'Don't be silly. People don't give presents to dead people.'

'Yes they do. I do.'

'Good afternoon, Omar Khayyám, your reverence, sir. On this silken rug I bow my head, humble in an obeisance to your vast wisdom, your unanswered questions. I would give you this offering, this small token of my esteem.'

'How do you do Mr. FitzGerald. I always wanted to meet you. I don't know anyone as brave as you. I made you this present. Mostly and most of all, I made this present for you. I hope you are pleased.

Good-bye Mr. FitzGerald,
Tamám Shud Omar Khayyám

Cécile E. Mactaggart
Hiniduma, Sri Lanka
1975

Willy Pogány's illustrations are reproduced through the kind permission of George G. Harrap and Co. Ltd. from the first translation of Edward FitzGerald's *Rubáiyát of Omar Khayyám* published in 1916.

Hodder and Stoughton kindly allowed the Edmund Dulac reproductions to be taken from the second translation of Edward FitzGerald's *Rubáiyát of Omar Khayyám* first published by them in June 1909 as their *Gift Book of the Year*.

This edition is limited to two thousand copies.

Though all my life I did delight to chase
Elusive wisdom from its secret place,
The learning that I learned was only this -
A nothingness within an empty space.

from a verse attributed to
Omar Khayyám